We

Minotaur

ARRANGED MONSTER MATES
EDEN EMBER

Cover & Editing by Perfectly Plotted Books

© 2023 Eden Ember
All rights reserved.
This work of fiction is intended for mature audiences only. All characters represented within are eighteen years of age or older and any resemblance to persons, living or dead, is purely coincidental. This work is property of Eden Ember, please do not reproduce illegally.

Chapter 1

Vrakius

A vision of beauty greeted me as I stepped into the Marriage Temple. She literally glowed with her creamy complexion and her eyes peered into mine as a slight smile stretched across her lovely face. Genetic matching did a superb job. I walked toward my future, my family, all as the magistrate rocked on his feet.

A few days ago I received word that the genetic database had found a match for me. Honestly, I had already figured my life was set as a loner meant for working the land. We came from Tariat in hopes of living fruitful, fulfilling lives. Tariat, a small planet in the Procyon System, had grown too small for the prolific minotaurs. The fact that the males outnumbered the females three to one also made it necessary to leave in order to find a mate.

Earth held promise as the indigenous beings there needed help after their near annihilation years before. There were plenty of human females to make up for the lack of minotaur females. Not only Tariat, but other planets and other alien species had come to rescue Earth in their time of need.

By the time I arrived on Earth to settle in

a minotaur territory in Alia Terra, the way was already paved. Animals of close relation to us were the very things we raised. Bovines walked on four legs and didn't communicate as intelligent beings, but were the food for the Earth dwellers. Part of me winced dearly at this, as the bovines, in particular the bulls, resemble my kind.

I laughed at the irony of it. The bovines were a hearty race of animals and provided food which ranked high in the food chain. But to my people, it was akin to cannibalism to eat the cattle we raised. The remedy was to bring the boarius from Tariat, and we each had several mating pairs to create our own food alongside the cattle. It worked, the boarius looking like some crossbreeding of cattle and pigs. The meat was similar to both beef and pork, according to the humans.

I watched my friends and kin receive their wives, one after the other. These beautiful creatures, called humans, fit in with our kind nearly perfectly. My hopes were dashed every time they ran the database and I wasn't called for a match, however. I'd given up and built my own home with a ranch the way I wanted it. Some of my kin continued to wait for their wives, but I wanted happiness in my surroundings as soon as possible.

"Vrakius, you're going to be sorry that you built your home. What if your wife doesn't like it?" Jorkais balked at my decision to build.

"As you can see, my kin, I have no wife of my own. How many rounds of checks have they done? Not all of our kind will find a wife. They told us it wasn't a guarantee."

His large hand landed on my shoulder. "I'm sorry for you."

But the call soon came and they told me they had a genetic match near enough to mine. I was to travel to north central Alia Terra, many miles from Taurus Terra.

I drove an old restored Earth vehicle to Central North Alia Terra to the marriage temple. It wasn't a hover vehicle, the sort that more affluent people possessed. Even so, I rather enjoyed steering over the old beat up roads. It gave me a closer view of what Earth had been at one time. When the aliens arrived, territories were claimed and vast amounts of land were left as we found it. Unlike the natives of this planet, we do not spoil land for the sake of destruction.

Taurus Terra had once been Texas, a large state in the country of the United States. When the aliens took over, including dignitaries from Tariat, they renamed it Alia Terra. A new Earth age began when we all arrived. Humankind was in a terrible way, destitute, starving, and under the iron fists of the rulers at that time. Their so-called one world government had failed quickly.

Spring time brought about the beauty of Earth as colorful flowers, flowering trees, and green grass and plants filled the landscape. The dormant trees came back to life with bright green leaves. Even the sky was soon again a deep blue with the occasional white clouds floating by. Some parts of Earth continued to reveal the true horrors that led to their dystopian age. Crumbling buildings, rats taking over, broken concrete, and nothing to count for to help a human survive framed the terrible conditions of the planet before my kind arrived to help.

My mate came from the East Coast of Terra Alia at such a place where the concrete was seen for miles and the state of health with these people was terrible. Illnesses ran rampant in these parts, the poor humans thin and emaciated.

The Marriage Temple appealed to both sides, the native Earthlings and the aliens who were looking for human mates. The genetic tests ensured a productive match. More than that, when the genes of our species lined up, many of the alien species reacted in the presence of their mates. We knew when we had found our mates. Humans did not, considering mating more as survival and a duty to simply procreate.

I had met many human females. They were lovely people, and they had an eagerness to survive and learn to fall in love with their mates. Luckily, fate intervened and most, if not all, fell completely in love with their prospective mates. I laughed at the term *wife* as used by humans. Minotaurs have always called them mates. On Earth there were traditions that the aliens adopted to help ease the humans into the new alien age. The Marriage Temples offered a safe location where both parties could come and connect in safety. The magistrate or priest would reside over the official ceremony, called a marriage or wedding ceremony. Once officially joined, we were able to take our new wives back to our homes to begin our lives with them.

I reached North Central, the place once a giant bustling city in the United States called Chicago, I believe. It had high fences to secure it from the rogue pirates who made their way from the southern territories occasionally to sack smaller towns. They were a lawless bunch, their home planet governed by anarchy. Arriving here helped them to find land and shelter from their once harried existence on their planet of Licentia, located near Tariat. A smaller and warmer planet, it was in constant upheaval.

"Vrakius Tarvir from Taurus Terra. I have an appointment at the Marriage Temple."

The tall alien nodded and smiled. "Here to pick up your new wife, eh?"

"Yes." My fingers gripped the steering wheel. These checkpoints were necessary, but they could also be a nuisance.

"Okay, your new wife's name is Auryn Ridgewood. She's already here and waiting for you." He shut the tablet and smiled as he opened his hand and motioned for me to enter through the gate.

Auryn Ridgewood. The name rolled off my tongue as if I had said it my entire life. I could only imagine what she looked like. Soft skin, lovely eyes. Just like all the wives of my kin in Taurus Terra. Not a single one of them caused my heart to resonate, which was good. My kin told me their hearts did so, once they had found their fated mates through the Marriage Temple.

Immediately, when my eyes peered upon the human female standing at the altar of the Marriage Temple, my body reacted. My heart pounded hard within my chest. Her hair resembled the same color as the top portion of the little cakes we eat back home. Chocolate, I think the humans called it. And her eyes were as blue as the dark blue sky outside. They were searching through the dim lighting at the temple for me. There was no doubt in my mind that she was the one for me.

The magistrate, clothed in his long robes with the ropes of honor hanging down the front of them, looked down at his tablet and then back up at me.

"Vrakius? Vrakius Tarvir, of Taurus Terra, of the minotaur clan?"

"Yes. And this is Auryn Ridgewood, my betrothed?" My voice boomed through the high ceilings of the temple.

Auryn blinked quickly as I approached. The air was filled with a palatable electricity. She blushed heavily as my eyes roamed over her soft, slender frame, taking in her curves and noting her flawless skin. She wore a well-fitting dress that made her look like royalty in my eyes. No one I had met on Earth could compare to her natural beauty. And when she locked eyes with me my breath caught. The entire world swam behind those blue orbs, and I had yet to even hear her voice.

"Vrakius, Auryn," the magistrate said as he waved at both of us.

"Vrakius." Auryn's voice filled me with rich desire, a passion that sparked wildly. I wanted to touch her, to rub the back of her soft hands.

"Auryn." I bowed in respect.

"Shall we begin?" The magistrate looked at the two of us. I nodded as did Auryn.

"Take her hand." The magistrate held up his tablet to begin the ceremony.

Auryn placed her hand in mind. I swayed as electricity passed between the two of us. Even she looked up at me in surprise.

"Very well, shall we begin?"

"Yes." I nodded.

"Yes, please," Auryn said and nodded as well.

And the words I've waited to hear since I landed on Earth finally reached my ears.

Chapter 2

Auryn

The door slammed when my little sister ran inside with the letter.

"A match, a match!" Chelsea waved the letter in the air.

"Who is it for?" I grabbed the letter and tore into it. My heart pounded for I knew my parents had sent in blood samples for all three of us sisters. While I wanted a better life, I didn't want to leave my family behind.

My eyes filled with tears as I read my name in the letter that stated they'd found the perfect genetic match for me. The letter crumbled in my grip as I turned to my younger sister. "Tell no one about this."

She shook her head. "But who got the match, Auryn? And you shouldn't keep it from me. It might be *me!*"

I held the letter above her head. "It's not about you. And it's none of your business."

My eighteen year old sister cried after me wanting to know who the letter was about.

"Agnes, then?"

I whirled around. "It's none of your business, Chelsea. Leave it at that."

The letter I took and hid behind my pillow. I shared a room with my two sisters, and being the oldest of the three I should be the first with a match. But having my blood sent to the DNA registry wasn't my idea. My parents thought it would be best, being that our living situation wasn't the greatest.

Large tears rolled from my eyes as my mother approached. She didn't get onto me like I had expected she would.

"We received a letter from the DNA registry."

I turned away, grinding the tears from my eyes with my hands. "Chelsea has a big mouth."

"Oh, darling, is it for you?"

A smile stretched across my face as I laughed sarcastically. "You think I would hide it from her or Agnes if it wasn't? They want this, but I do not."

My mother's tender hand brushed my cheek. "My dear Auryn. We have lived such an incredibly difficult life. Going for days without food, taking turns eating the meals…it's no life for you. If you wish to make things easier for us, you will go and marry your match. You will allow us to have more food by doing so. And you will thrive by going as well. Happiness and fulfillment awaits you at the Marriage Temple. They will send a train ticket to go to North Central. It's your destiny, sweetie."

"Oh, mother," I turned to her while crying. "You and papa deserve a better future."

"Papa and I deserve to see our daughters make it in life, happy and taken care of. Whoever it is, you have a chance of being healthy and happy. Go, and don't look back, Auryn. Promise me."

"I promise." We hugged. She squeezed me tightly, growing stronger while knowing that her eldest daughter had the correct genetic match to an alien.

"We are proud of you and very happy." Papa kept a brave face as they took me to the train station. Agnes and Chelsea were jealous, though. They wanted to go instead. In all fairness, I was the oldest and deserved the first match, anyway. Even if I wasn't all that happy about it to begin with.

"Do not come back, you hear?" Mother knew me well. She knew I'd consider taking the first opportunity to come back.

"Swear it, Auryn. Do us this last favor, and don't let us down. Stay with your match." Papa pulled the ultimate and made me swear to it.

"Brave face, Auryn. Do you have the dress we got you?"

I nodded. Mother had saved and bought each of us a special dress for when we received our call to the Marriage Temple.

My sisters gave me a stiff hug, jealousy oozing from their pores.

"Oh, don't worry. You'll get a letter soon. If I did, you will. It means our genetic matches are out there."

Agnes threw her arms around me tightly. "I hope I get a minotaur, too, and can come to Taurus Terra."

Chelsea grinned. "I really don't care who or where, I'd just like to have an adventure."

After the promise I made to them, I took one last

look at my family. Only if my new alien husband decided to take me on a trip to see my parents would I see them again. I squared my shoulders, took a deep breath and boarded the train. I didn't look back.

Seeing Alia Terra from the window of the old train brought on a sense of adventure. Adventure like Chelsea wanted. Agnes, Chelsea and I were born in the region of Alia Terra near the seashore in a place that was once called Maryland. Now it's simply Alia Terra District 852. It's where the humans concentrated when the aliens landed years before my birth.

The farther away from the east I traveled, the more optimistic I became about my new life. Like it or not, I had to do it for my family and for myself. There was a wonderful minotaur out there who had requested a human mate through a DNA match.

The train pulled into North Central station and all sorts of beings, including other human females, exited the train. Some were dressed with beautiful gowns, while others wore the same worn-out clothing they had worn most of their lives. My mother saved to buy the dresses for her daughters. She crocheted little pot holders and sold them in the flea markets as often as she could. I smoothed my dress, feeling particularly beautiful. In fact, I felt almost like royalty; a princess.

"Marriage Temple!" An alien called from the curb, a bus waited there to take us to the temple.

I counted eight females as well as myself who boarded the bus. The city laid out before us, a mixture of old crumbling buildings from the days of old and the newer space-age buildings built with alien technology.

When we finally arrived, we were escorted to a large room where we filled out paperwork and were told to wait. Each of us were nervous, but excited. I listened to the horror stories some of these women had about where they came from. Many didn't have families like I did. My heart went out to them for such terrible circumstances.

I shook my head and pushed the sad thoughts about the family I left behind out of my head. Ahead of me was the promise of a new life, a love, a new family. Many aliens walked through the halls, all of them different. I didn't see any minotaurs, though. One by one, the ladies were called to the temple center where the altar was and the priest or magistrate performed the ceremonies.

The waiting gave me time to calm my nerves. For the first time in my life I was in for a big change. My mother and father had an arranged marriage as well, back when the aliens were first taking over with the new governments. Their parents were very strict about making certain it was a human with human marriage. Since the alien invasion, the human population has dwindled, though. Now with an abundance of male aliens in need of mates, the DNA registry has helped to remedy this problem by mixing humans with aliens.

"Auryn Ridgewood."

I stood tall, sucked in a deep breath, and followed

the woman through the temple. She smiled at me as she walked, leading the way. The long hall echoed with each footstep.

The double doors to the temple opened as a couple of alien guards stepped to the side to allow us entry. My eyes widened as I looked at the vastness of the room, including high ceilings, great columns, and a few rows of seats facing the massive stone altar. The setup was intended to represent all the deities of both humans and aliens. The magistrate smiled as I approached. He was a tall alien with a large head and a magistrate garb who stood in front of the altar. An official recorder who made certain the paperwork was in order sat at a desk off to the right.

The magistrate rocked on his feet as we stood, looking toward the double doors that were now closed. He glanced at the ornate clock that was dropping sand through the gears, causing it to tick off the seconds.

"Is Vrakius Tarvir here?"

"He's entered North Center, Magistrate. He's caught at the gates as there are many in the city."

My heart pounded. What if he decided not to show? What if he changed his mind? My eyes teared up thinking he'd left me at the altar even before seeing me.

Suddenly, the doors jarred and the guards pulled the handles, opening them wide. The most beautiful creature I'd ever seen strode through them, a look of pure intention upon his face as he walked with great presence and dignity across the room. His eyes were on me, and they looked over my body from my head to my toes and back up again. When he peered into my eyes, I shivered with anticipation. He had muscles built upon muscles, yet was very human in appearance with exception to the horns growing out of his head. I could see us together.

"Gather your hands." His hands opened before me and I slid mine into his. An instant shot of electricity passed between us, the warmth of it crawling up my arm to my neck and resulting in a deep blush over my face.

The ceremony was quick with a handful of promises uttered. Then it was done. The recorder pressed the seal onto the official document, of which we received a copy while a copy would go to the central marriage database.

"You are husband and wife," the magistrate said as he bowed before us.

Chapter 3

Vrakius

Auryn's soft hands made my heart strum harder while the aroma of her feminine uniqueness caused my body to stiffen with extreme desire. However, I maintained my composure as we took the marriage oath and the papers were signed and sealed.

Auryn, a vision of pure beauty, smiled as we stood near a temple column for a photo. I looked deeply into her eyes, ready to lose myself into her arms forever.

"Vrakius, you are wed. You both may go." The magistrate broke eye contact between the two of us. I smiled and let her hands fall.

She slid her hand through my arm as we exited the temple as husband and wife. Once outside, I led her to the old truck. She giggled as her hand ran over the rusted paint.

"I believe these were a big deal to the humans of the past. Where did you find it?"

I chuckled at her enthusiasm and delighted in her knowledge of history. "It was left on my land. I acquired an old ranch from the early years. Minotaurs are agricultural creatures, though it is a bit odd to have cattle on my ranch."

"Oh, I haven't thought of that. You being a minotaur and owning cattle. Is it true then, that you are closely related to both humans and cattle?"

"Most likely to some degree we are genetically similar to cattle. To humans as well." I took her hand into mine and brought it to my lips. "I have read on how to win the love of a human female."

Auryn smiled, her eyes gazing into mine. "I'm sure it won't be that difficult if you keep this up."

We left in the old truck with North Central behind us. I didn't know a lot about my new wife, other than she certainly struck my heart when I first saw her. "Are you from a city or the countryside?"

Her chin lifted as she looked out the window. "The city. An old city of the United States, torn into shambles where the poorest of the poor live among the last of the human families."

The urge to pull over and claim her was growing stronger. We had a long way to go to get home and being out between territories was quite risky. Rogue pirates roamed the land, snatching humans whenever they could. This made it dangerous for us to stop for any length of time along the road. I would make certain to keep a keen eye on her.

"Are we driving straight back? The train ride was nice," she mused, looking out the window.

I took her hand. "A train ride would have been nice, as I could have paid more attention to you than having to keep an eye on the road."

We bumped along, the old road not being so

merciful as it was in dire need of repair. One bump jarred Auryn greatly.

"Yes, it would be nice to have your full attention. I'm not used to driving in these antique vehicles. We did a lot of walking back east. We didn't even own a vehicle. We took the shuttles if we needed to go very far, and the train if we needed to go farther."

My mate deserved attention from me. We had just met and married. Thankfully, we were coming upon a territory of friendlies where I could keep an eye out for an inn or a hotel. *River's Inn* was perched alongside a long, wide river as we pulled up.

"Oh, are we stopping here? This is the Mississippi River, the longest river in Alia Terra."

I laughed. "Yes, I will see if they have a vacancy. We need time to rest."

Auryn shyly looked down, giggling. "Rest?" Her brow lifted endearingly. I blushed at the implication.

"Yes, and to get to know each other." While I wanted to claim her, I was not so quick to show this as I had just met her. Intimacy would be forthcoming and expected. Not only by us, but by the fact we were married at the Marriage Temple. And soon, a pregnancy, a baby, would be expected if both of us have healthy reproductive organs. According to our genetics and physical exams, this was the case.

We settled into a room, and she coyly smiled before disappearing into the bathroom. I heard the shower running and sat back to wait patiently for her to emerge. When she finally came out, I smiled.

Nothing but a white fluffy towel covered Auryn's body. Her skin glistened from being washed, and her scent, raw and fresh, caused my body to react.

"Your turn." She said with a grin.

I walked to the bathroom. I had not planned on taking a shower, but perhaps it would make her feel better.

"Only if you promise to stay dressed in the towel." My brow lifted playfully.

Her giggle sent me scurrying into the bathroom to shower quickly. I didn't waste a second and instead of wearing a towel, I proudly stepped out in all my naked glory. Minotaurs are a proud people, and we enjoy our bodies. I want my wife to see what she's got.

"Oh my. Wow. You are a right gorgeous man." Her eyes swung to my cock, which stood on end, fully engorged, bobbing, and wanting her.

I stepped toward Auryn and took hold of her shoulders before leaning in and pressing my lips to hers in a sweet feathery kiss. She moaned, her arms going around my neck, pressing her body against mine. Our tongues touched, sending electricity through my belly and straight to my cock. Pressing in, I pulled her fully to me, my hands moving down her back and rubbing her soft skin.

Auryn stepped back, a smile stretching across her lovely face. Her hands moved over my belly and up my chest, stroking my muscles, making gooseflesh appear on my skin. I tugged on her towel until it loosened and fell from her body. An amazing creature of sexy curves, feminine fragrance, and alluring brown eyes captivated me. She had the sweetest smile I had ever seen. I drew in a deep breath as I beheld her wonderful beauty.

"I've never seen a creature as beautiful as you. And you're mine!" My eyes danced over the mounds on her chest, the nipples growing so hard that they puckered the skin around them. Reaching out, I tenderly touched her, brushing the tips of my fingers over her soft, smooth skin, tracing a line from her ear and down her neck to her shoulders. Kneeling before her wide-eyed, I took in all she had to offer. My hands moved to her chest, each one landing on a breast. Her breath caught as I gently squeezed. Leaning in, I kissed her lips once again.

Auryn moaned, her hands moving around my back, nails digging into my flesh as she pressed her naked body to mine. I wanted to explore her, get to know her better, before I claimed her. Leaning back, I smiled and gazed at her chest. Slowly, I leaned in and my lips lightly kissed and teased a nipple. Her arms wrapped around me tighter, pulling me to her.

I moved to the other breast and sucked the nipple between my lips. Her head rolled back as she moaned again, this time with a huskiness. Auryn leaned into and kissed my neck, playfully kissing my ear, her hands gripping my horns, pulling me to her.

I stood and hoisted her into my arms and walked to the bed. As I laid her on it, she smiled and scooted back to the pillows.

"I'm yours, Vrakius. You can have me. You can

take me and you don't have to be gentle."

I smiled. My body hummed with such a fierce desire that I could easily do as she requested.

I leaned over her and kissed the nape of her neck. "No, my wife. I want to take my time getting to know you. I want to taste every bit of your soft body. I want to see what makes you hum."

She giggled. "It's between my legs, my love, my minotaur."

Her legs opened, revealing her sweetness to me, the soft slit glistening with juices, the hardening knob at the top of the mound pushing forth for attention. I had read about human female anatomy. Auryn's slight frame didn't look like it could take the bigness of me, but I was willing to try.

I hovered over her, smelling and kissing my way down, paying extra attention to her nipples. She really seemed to like that. *Noted.* Moving down, her hands rubbed over my horns, and through my hair. Her legs opened wide, welcoming me as I settled between her knees.

My tongue licked through her soft warm slit, the juices there sweet and tasty. My cock intensified in girth and length as I kissed the outer lips. Prodding forth, I licked the entrance to her sweet tunnel, and she moaned and yelped. Lifting up, I eyed her as she spoke to me.

"I've never done anything before. I'm a virgin and you're my first."

Oh! This caused a frenzy of desire to flood into my belly, my body trembling at the thought of claiming her fresh, pure, virgin opening. When my tongue reached the swelling member, she nearly lost it, and her breath sucked in so quickly. Auryn's hands held me in place.

"Yes! Yes, that's the spot!"

I leaned in, bearing down with my tongue over her hardness, licking down and prodding over her very small, very tight closed hole. The virgins have to be broken into, a layer of hymen blocking me. She didn't seem to mind as I stuck my tongue around it and through it.

Her bottom ground into the mattress, her breaths coming in short hits, and she clung to my horns, keeping me firmly at her sweet spot. The more I licked, the more juices flowed, which I lapped up. Tasty sweet flavor filled my senses and she craved to give me even more. Auryn's sweet body trembled, her breathing picking up, and while she arched her back she yelped out as pleasure flooded through her. My tongue stayed on the hard little member as it quivered, and she rocked through the waves of pleasure. I did this until Auryn pushed me back, her hands on my horns, and then moved up farther on the pillows to get away from me.

"I didn't hurt you, did I?"

She laughed. "Do you honestly think I was moaning and yelling out of pain? Oh no, Vrakius, you took me to such heights of pleasure I didn't know existed until today."

Chapter 4

Auryn

My head swam dizzily as I came down from the euphoria caused by Vrakius' tongue. The minotaur certainly knew how to please a woman. I grinned at him as I opened my arms. He had to be careful with me because of his horns. He was very human-like except for the horns, which certainly set him apart from men on Earth.

"My sweet wife, I really enjoyed watching you as the pleasure took hold."

"I have a question." I giggled. He knew about my virginity and I wondered about him.

"Anything."

"Have you ever been with someone? Like this?"

This time he laughed. "No. I took time to read about it, though. I wanted to make certain I could please a female human."

"Well, whatever book you read, *damn*."

"So, I did it correctly, then?"

"Oh, yes. You did it like you're a minotaur with great sexual experience."

He hovered over me and our lips met again, this time I tasted myself as he kissed me. His rock solid body pressed against mine, his cock demanding attention. I reached down and touched it, still rock hard to grip. Vrakius moaned and lurched forward as my hand moved along his girthy member.

"Now, it's my turn to explore you." I pushed him onto his back. I wanted the same opportunity to get to know his body as he had with mine.

He laid back on the pillows, his eyes firmly planted on me. I raised up, hovering over him before lowering myself until our lips met. This time I was in charge. My hands moved over his big shoulders and down his arms. My lips kissed his cheek and then made their way to his neck, and down. He smelled wonderful, a mixture of woodsy and mossy with a hint of musk. It drove me wild and I wanted to consume him with my lips.

His skin felt like velvet, yet rugged at the same time. Lightly bronzed, as if he had a healthy tan, he was smooth to the touch. My lips wandered over his neck and to his chest. I loved his muscle definition. It was as if he worked out all the time. Little taut nipples greeted me as I moved my lips over them, my tongue teasing each one. Vrakius moaned, his arms encircling me, holding me tightly. I loved it.

My lips kissed ever downward as I scooted back. Thick thighs opened for me, and his male package, *oh my!* Girthy and long, his cock bobbed at me angrily, a deep red with a dot of precum on the very tip. I leaned down, my tongue licking it, tasting the saltiness of it. Then my lips opened and I moved my hand down the length of his manhood. So thick he was that I could barely squeeze my lips over the top.

Vrakius' hands moved up to my head, holding me there, enjoying it.

I sucked more precum from the tip. Vrakius lost himself in my attention, his groans becoming louder as he thrusted his cock into my mouth, wanting it to slide in farther, but I wasn't certain I could do it. I gagged and sat back, laughing.

"I'm so sorry. You're just so big. I think this will take some practice from me."

He sat up, his arms pulling me to him. "It's okay. And I don't want you to finish me like this. I want you, Auryn. I want to make you mine in every way possible."

I slid down onto the pillows and trembled with excitement. My husband, my minotaur, crawled between my legs. I lifted one and he grabbed it and kissed each toe. I squirmed and giggled because it tickled. My other leg went around his waist. My eyes closed as he took hold of his giant cock and rubbed it gingerly through my soft warm folds. He swirled it over my clit, causing heat to flood into my pelvis once again.

Before I got off, he slid to the opening and slowly pushed his way in. A tearing sensation caused me to cry out from the pain of my hymen breaking.

"Oh, I'm so sorry." Vrakius pulled back as I whimpered.

I grabbed him immediately. "No, it's okay. It is to be expected with a first time virgin. You just have to shove it in and do it. My body will stretch and open. And there may be some blood. I'm sorry if that puts you off, perhaps I can break it myself and then we can do it."

"No, I will be slow and gentle with you. I don't like causing pain for my love, though."

Vrakius moaned as he slowly pushed in. I bit my lower lip to keep from whimpering and turned my head, closing my eyes. *Breathe through the pain, it's worth it in the end.* He slowly filled my tunnel, stretching me, tearing into me. It hurt, but I kept my lip between my teeth because I wanted him to enjoy it. I wanted him to claim me as his wife, his fated mate. I could do this!

My body soon reacted with pleasure flowing slowly into my pelvis. Though the entrance to my tunnel was torn and I was sure I was bleeding, he moved his thick cock in and out of my tightness, the pain disappearing. My hands clung to him, my nails digging into his back.

"Auryn. My sweet Auryn. The sun and the moon and the stars all rise and set on you. You are the center of my universe. My everything. I shall give you all that I have. Everything." His face skewed in pleasure as he peered into my eyes and leaned in to kiss me deeply while pumping into me faster and faster.

I whimpered and moaned, the pain and the pleasure intermingling in a strange erotic way. I wanted him to finish inside me, to take me, to claim me. Everything in my world tuned into him. It was as if he had lassoed my heart and tucked it neatly inside, our souls touching, becoming one. Yes, he was my soulmate, the one I was born to please. Light flooded into my soul as the pain left and pleasure surmounted over me once again.

He sawed fast and hard, and I moved with him, enjoying the new sensations rocking throughout my body. Stars flared before my eyes as my body succumbed to the powerful orgasm. I grabbed hold and clung to him as I lost control of myself. My body shook as pleasure soared through me.

"Oh, Auryn, I'm taking you. You're mine, now and forever." Vrakius heaved his body forward, thrusting as I was still in the throes of passion, he came as well. The two of us rocked through the endless waves of pleasure until we had nothing more to give.

Vrakius rolled off of me, breathless and thoroughly spent. I relaxed on the pillow, catching my breath while holding his hand. Laughter bubbled out of me. The sheer oddness of meeting someone for the first time earlier that day, and then making love to them with such intensity made me laugh.

I looked at him, my head rolling to the side. He turned to me, his eyes so deeply blue and pure and filled with love. His hand brushed against my cheek. "How are you doing, my love?"

I rolled toward him, my arm wrapping around his arm. "I am wonderful. I've never in my life…*wow*."

Then I looked down and saw the blood between my legs. It was proof of my virginity.

Vrakius sat up quickly, his eyes wide. "I have hurt you. I'm so, so sorry, my love." His head shook.

I quickly sat up as well, taking his chin into my

hand and shaking my head. "No, love, you didn't hurt me. It happens to all female virgins. Well, *human* female virgins, the first time. And believe me, it was so worth it. Now, after I heal, it will just get better and better."

His expression of sorrow made me want to cry. I wrapped my arms around him.

"It's so odd. I know we just met, but it feels like we've known each other for years."

"It is proof that you are my fated mate. That's how minotaurs know. We take a look at our mate and know the instant we see them."

I took his hand and smiled. "Is that how you felt about me when you saw me?"

"Isn't it obvious? Yes, of course. The genetic database has never made a mistake. I have no regrets. I am looking forward to taking you back to Taurus Terra to begin our lives together. I only hope you will enjoy it as much as I will. I understand you left your family behind, but that doesn't mean you'll never see them again. Perhaps someday I'll take you east to visit them. You can stay in touch with them as well."

"My life is with you now. Me leaving my family behind helped them a great deal. They have more room and more food now. With me there it was a struggle. Of course, my two sisters are also waiting for their letters from the Registry."

"If you and I are a match, that means they'll find their matches, too."

"Perhaps with a minotaur?" I smiled hopefully.

"That would be wonderful. But I can't guarantee that. However, we'll track them and hopefully get to visit them soon."

I nodded, realizing that he left his home to come to Earth. "What about you? Is your family here or back on your home planet?"

"Minotaurs consider ourselves kin. In a strange way, we consider the bovines we farm as distant relatives. We don't eat beef, by the way. If you want beef, I can get you some, but we have our own boarius herd that gives us the meat we enjoy from our home planet."

I laughed. "Wow. I never really thought of it that way. I've eaten so many alien foods that I find I can adjust easily to what's offered. We were hungry a lot back home."

Vrakius frowned. "I hate hearing that. The plight of your people is sad. Some of the aliens seek to take advantage by putting you into servitude. And others, like my people, seek only wives. I wish we could have your family come to live in Taurus Terra, but that's not possible."

"It's okay, really. We had the opportunity to join the Alien Service, but we chose our freedom, some semblance of the old times. It comes at a cost though. But we survived and now that I'm here with you, my family will have it better." I squeezed his hand, hoping he'd realize I was in this with him by my choice.

Chapter 5

Vrakius

My beautiful mate pulled at my heart like no other being on this planet. I never imagined having my life centered around someone else. The ferocity to protect her went beyond my protection of my farm, or kin. Auryn became my life, my love, my mate.

Auryn frowned. "I hate that our honeymoon is over so quickly, but I understand. Life needs our attention, as well as the ranch that you have. I can't wait to see it and to step into the role of being your wife."

"*Honeymoon* is a new term for me. On Tariat, we find our fated mates, much like when we met, only we're not in a temple. We have a bonding ceremony that same day, if agreed, and we move right into working our lives."

"Were you a rancher on Tariat?" Her kind eyes peered up at me.

"I was into agriculture, yes. Overpopulation and not enough females sent us looking throughout the galaxy for a place to grow and expand. We actually tested our blood to find who might be a close genetic match with humans. Only those who were close enough came to Earth."

Auryn slipped her hand into mine, her small fingers curling around my hand. "And I'm glad you did."

"Me too. But I'm sorry about the honeymoon time. We'll be together every night which certainly puts a big smile on my face." I brought her hand to my lips and kissed the back of it.

The old truck trundled down the broken road heading south. There wasn't much to see along the way, except for the expanse of territories of other aliens and their lands. Many farmed while many had ranches. Humans told us Earth had gone backwards in a way back to more basic times, but things were once again moving forward with aliens coming to Earth to live. It was all coming more into balance.

We drove into Taurus Terra and were greeted by a smoky haze. I looked toward the skies and did not see any rain clouds overhead. After turning onto another road a roadblock suddenly stopped us.

"The South-Taupis are at it again," the male minotaur standing guard said as he looked into the truck.

"I'm Vrakius, this is my new wife, Auryn. They have crossed our border again?"

"Jerakan. Yes, they breached the boundary and have stolen the wives and half-human children from several of our communities. We're gathering a group to go take them back."

"We need order. This isn't a way to live." My fingers curled into fists.

"What's happening?" Auryn asked with a worried look settling upon her beautiful face.

"The South-Taupis are aliens from Taupi'Sau. They haven't come here in agreement with the other species who live on Earth to live in peace. They've claimed the territory just to our south, so we call them the South-Taupis. They kidnap our humans, wanting them for themselves."

"That's awful. What can we do to help?" Auryn bent forward while looking at Jerakan. I loved that about her, the willingness to help without knowing all the facts. And yet, here I was bringing a human female into dangerous territory.

"They've set fields on fire as diversions and then the men ran to put it out, they scooped up the wives and children."

"I see the haze from the fires. We've got to do something to stop this."

"We are. We are gathering the minotaur army along with the group of concerned citizens and we've requested help from the others in our region to help, because once these pirates exhaust Taurus Terra they'll go after them as well. Some examples will be made of them when we find them."

"As in prison?" Auryn asked.

"Yes, we're looking at the islands off the coast and building a prisons there. Also, they could be sent off-planet if they continue this conduct. But first, we must save ours, then we will imprison those who did it. We will warn the others to either comply with the laws of the land, or leave. This behavior won't be allowed here."

"Thank God! I want to help those who are searching."

I turned to her, my mouth stretching into a thin line. "Auryn, they want *you*. They want all beings like you. It's dangerous being here at all." My head shook.

"We have a caravan going around and helping those in need. You could start there. And Auryn's welcome to hide in the back of it to avoid detection."

I nodded and looked at my new wife. "Are you okay with doing that?"

"I guess I'll have to be. I don't want them kidnapping me, but I want to help." She's adamant about helping in this situation.

We climbed inside the caravan and she slipped into the back in between boxes of supplies. Our journey went south, and then we turned and went northwest. Jerakan drove the caravan and nodded to the back.

"She's not safe where we're going if she's spotted." His thick brow lifted. "I've sent my wife and daughter north to her family until this is settled.

I nodded, understanding what he was suggesting. Looking back at Auryn, she stared out the window with wide eyes taking in the land as we drove.

"I need to talk with Auryn. I'll have to take her east to her family, though. They're not close by here."

"We have another caravan waiting at the northern border down from where you entered that's taking off and heading east. They can get her to her family over there."

I crawled to the back of the caravan as Jerakan turned north again. After shifting a box to the floor I sat down beside my new wife.

"This is a nice surprise. I love having you with me." She grabbed my hands and hugged them making it even harder for me to tell her the plan.

"Auryn, my first priority is to make certain you are safe. Right now, until we apprehend these pirates and stop the kidnappings and field burnings, Taurus Terra isn't a safe place for you."

She shook my hands. "I know. I plan to stay stuck to you the entire time."

I shook my head. "I'm taking you to another caravan that's heading east. They will take you back to your family."

Instantly, tears sprang to her eyes. "What? *No!* We just got married. I can't go back to my family. I just can't. Please, Vrakius, don't send me away." Tears fell from her eyes and then rolled off her chin.

"Oh, love, it's not that I *want* to send you away. I'm doing it for your safety. I will come for you as soon as it's safe here."

"No, please. Please don't send me back to my family. It's a hardship on them, a burden. I can't go!"

"My love, you must. It's too dangerous here."

"Not if I stay with you the entire time. I promise I won't leave your side. Please don't send me away. My heart can't take it."

I took a slow, calm breath, because everything

within me wanted to do nothing more than to please her. "I promise, as soon as the situation has become better I will come for you."

"I have no choice, then? I can't decide this for myself?"

"It's not that I want to command you to do anything, Auryn. I want to keep you safe and I will do what I can to keep you safe. That's it right there."

She nodded and grew stoic, her head turning to the window on the other side. I put my arm around her and hugged her. She looked up at me and I leaned in, brushing my lips on hers. Her hands grabbed my arms.

"I thought we were honeymooning, even at home? Just one night is all we had."

"I know. I hate it, too. I promise I'll come for you."

I stood and made my way back to the front of the caravan.

"You know, it might be safer for Auryn to stay here. I sent my wife away because of our toddler daughter."

I glanced back at Auryn. She still faced the window with a forlorn look on her face. "I am doing what's best for her. If they took her and harmed her, I wouldn't hold back my wrath. She means everything to me and I won't lose her. I just found her."

Jerakan laughed. "I understand."

We stopped for food at a small establishment. I smiled at Auryn. "Now you can try boarius."

"Yeah." Her depressed tone sent chills down my

spine.

"Love, please know that I want you safe. You are much safer there on the east coast with your family than you are here right now. Had I known this would happen, I wouldn't have brought you back here."

She smiled, her mood lightening. "Then let's go back north. Let's have the honeymoon and come back when it's safe."

I looked down. "I can't leave my kin like this, and my ranch needs me back. My full intentions were to bring you to the ranch with me and we would get on with life. But this is happening and I'll not leave them in their time of need."

"Can't you see? I want to help too! Please, Vrakius, let me stay with you. I can't leave you, not now, not when we just found each other."

She broke my heart. I pulled her into my arms and held her against me. The joy we had that morning was quickly fleeting and yet will have to do for the foreseeable future.

We had grilled boarius with stewed root vegetables seasoned with fresh herbs.

"It is good. I'd like to stay here and eat more of this. And oddly, it's very much like lean pork."

Jerakan laughed. "That's what we're told. You know, we've even started a market for it outside of Taurus Terra."

"Yes, and I have a large herd along with the bovine," I said.

"You two make it sound so wonderful here," Auryn said with a hint of sadness.

Chapter 6

Auryn

Vrakius wanted to get rid of me. Well, okay, maybe not get *rid* of me because he doesn't like me, but to keep me safe. We climbed back into the caravan after eating dinner.

"Jerakan, do you think these South-Taupis are going into other territories as well as here?"

He nodded. "Oh, I'm certain they are. They've gone west of us."

"I'm sure it's just a matter of time before they do. That's why it's so important to stop them." Vrakius turned back to look at me.

I looked down, defeated. "But what if they go *east?* What if they find out there's a caravan of humans heading east and they decide to capture us?Then you'll never know how to find me." I didn't own a wrist comm as I had been too poor. Vrakius had one, but what good would it be to me if he lost me?

Vrakius's brow furrowed. "I know, that could happen. But there's safety in numbers. And the minotaurs are driving the caravan."

"Then you drive it." I bounced to the seat directly behind the driver and passenger. There wasn't much room, but I perched on the edge of the seat, hoping to talk some sense into him.

Vrakius looked desperately at Jerakan. "Could I?"

"I'm sorry, we already have drivers and a full caravan with the addition of Auryn now. You're needed here."

I took Vrakius's arm. "Then just let me fight alongside you. Maybe I could disguise myself as a female minotaur. Surely, they aren't much taller than me. Or maybe they'd think of me as a teenage minotaur. I could find some horns."

Vrakius shook his head. "Love, please stop. I won't risk it. As much as you think you could stay by my side, it won't be possible all the time. I'll worry less about you knowing you were heading back east. I have your parents' address. It will all work out in the end."

Tears filled my eyes. "Please, Vrakius. I don't want to leave you. Not now. I have a bad feeling about it." I couldn't describe why, but my gut was telling me not to get on that other caravan and head east. I wasn't sure if it had to do with me or with him.

There was nothing I could do, no way of convincing him otherwise. Vrakius locked on with Jerakan's description of the situation and agreed that sending me east was the best thing they could do for me. I'd rather hide out somewhere near the territory than to go back to my parents. It was hard enough leaving them in the first place and to do it again…I just don't want to go through that.

Jerakan looked at Vrakius and pulled into a park. "Take your time. The caravan isn't leaving for a while."

"What's going on?" I asked as he grabbed my hand and we walked into the park. "What is this place?"

"Minotaur territory offers parks for those traveling and arriving. A place to have a rest stop, to let the livestock have a moment to graze, or to let out their pets."

"Why are we here?" I cried as we topped a small hill.

He stopped and turned to me, backing me against a tree. No one else was around. His arms slid around my shoulders. "Because we needed a moment before you head east and I head into Taurus to take care of the pirates." Before I could answer, his lips brushed against mine.

I entwined my arms around his muscled neck, breathing in his masculine scent, desire flaming within my loins. He was my new husband, dammit. We should be at each other's side every night, basking in the afterglow of raw lovemaking, enjoying each other. But instead, the damn pirates had to ruin it by kidnapping the wives and children of his kin.

He groaned, pulling me up to meet with his throbbing cock. My hand slid down his pants and grasped his thick member, squeezing it. His hands pulled up my dress and yanked down the panties underneath. I didn't care as I stepped out of them, leaving the pair on the ground. He undid his pants and pulled out his giant cock.

It was like a scene from one of the ancient

romance books I had read back home. We actually lived in an old library converted into a tiny apartment, and the bookshelves remained with the books. It provided the walls that separated our room from our parents and from the small living space. My sisters and I devoured the books we had on the shelves, providing us with escapes to other worlds and other times.

His lips trailed down my neck as he hoisted me into his arms. My legs wrapped around him as I looked around quickly and made certain no one was around watching. It was as if fate cleared this part of the park just for us. The only sounds were the wind blowing in the tops of the trees and a stream bubbling nearby.

My lips met with his and into my muff he pressed his cock. It stretched and tore me a little again, but I didn't care nor did I whimper. I just wanted Vrakius inside me. This moment we were one, we moved as one, our bodies climbing with waves of pleasure slowly washing over us. His cock moved in and out of me, his moans increasing.

He kissed me with fervor, his tongue dipping into my mouth, darting at my tongue. I gave back the same fervor he gave me. I wanted him to miss me, to realize how good we were together.

His cock sawed against my clit, and I moved in unison with him for the greatest sensation. My head swirled with dizziness as I clung to my new husband, our lives melting into one, until I exploded in his arms, moving quickly while waves of pleasure rushed through my pelvis. I'm certain my moans were so loud that even Jerakan heard that, but at that moment I didn't care.

Two seconds later, Vrakius gripped me harder, moving faster, filling my tunnel with his seed. We rocked through the waves of pleasure, moving as one, moaning and clinging to one another until it subsided.

With him still embedded inside me, we locked eyes and leaned in, kissing. Slowly, he pulled out and gently set me back onto the ground. I quickly grabbed my panties and yanked them up and smoothed my dress.

"Thank you, my love. I wish we could do this again tonight in the comfort of our bed, but it will have to wait."

I sadly nodded and turned because Jerakan was waiting nearby. Nothing I could say would change Vrakius's mind anyway. Before I took another step, he took my arm and wheeled me around until I was facing him.

"Auryn, you really are my life now. Please understand why I want to keep you safe by sending you east. I promise I will come for you as soon as the pirates here are handled." His eyes looked intently into mine and didn't waver. He meant what he said, but I didn't agree with his decision to send me back. All I could do was nod my understanding.

"Even if I have a bad feeling about us parting company today?"

He considered my face for a moment. "I think you

are concerned, but worry not. I will come for you very soon."

I smiled into his face, then leaned in for another quick kiss. I didn't express my thoughts and went along with him because I didn't want an argument. He squeezed me to him as we walked back to the caravan and headed northeast.

We pulled into the station at the border where the caravan waited for me, steam puffing from behind it. Inside were three women and two children along with two minotaurs. All were wide-eyed and scared. I set my bag on a seat and turned back to Vrakius, flinging myself into his arms.

"It's okay, my love. We will be together soon, I promise. I'm very relieved you are heading back east." We kissed one last time and said goodbye before I turned to go back inside.

After I crawled into the caravan, I sat beside a woman with her small child between us. She smiled at me.

"Newly married?"

I nodded. "Day before yesterday. Coming home and then we were faced with this." I splayed my hands, my mouth in a frown.

"I'm Catharine, by the way. And this is little Ellie," she said as she smiled down at the little girl.

I gazed at the child, a girl who had horn buds peeking out of her hair.

"I'm Auryn. And my husband is Vrakius. I hate this."

"I know. I do, too. This is the second time my

husband T'koi has sent us away."

The scenery soon flew by the window as we were leaving Taurus Terra behind. It soon seemed as if we were in safer territory as the journey progressed.

"Where are you heading, by the way? My daughter and I are heading to the Smoky Mountains, to a hidden getaway T'koi and I have there. It's surrounded by smaller, safer villages."

"That's nice. My parents are in Sector 800's on the coast." Oh, how I'd go for an invitation to her little getaway and not have to see my parents. That would be wonderful, but she didn't extend it and since I had just met her I would not ask.

The more I thought about it, the more I felt that sticking around closer to Taurus Terra was important. I couldn't put my finger on why I felt so strongly, but my gut instinct kicked in and was telling me not to stray too far from there. My drop off point was the farthest away and I didn't want to be a burden on anyone.

We stopped after an hour's driving because the little kids had to go to the bathroom. It was a perfect out for me. I exited the caravan and followed Catharine into the store.

"Listen, please tell the drivers I'm going back to Taurus Terra. My husband needs me and I just don't feel right heading east. I don't have a little kid to worry about or I would."

She grabbed my arm. "Are you sure you want to do that, Auryn? It's dangerous here."

"Not here," I said as I waved my hands. "Here it is

safe. It's down in the minotaur territory and west of there that the pirates are heading. Don't worry about me. Just tell the driver right before he takes off and please, don't come looking for me. I gotta run."

"Okay, you know what's best for you," she said as she watched me walk out of the little store and head back to the old road by foot.

Chapter 7

Vrakius

It took everything I had not to stop Jerakan and chase Auryn down. Could she have come with me? She begged and begged. My heart ripped in two when the caravan drove away with her.

"Looks like they may be here," Jerakan said as we turned down a road with heavy smoke billowing in the sky ahead of us. *No, Auryn is in the best place which is away from here.*

We pulled off the road and ran on foot to the fires in the field. While others were putting out the fires there, Jerakan and I rushed to the home. The wife and children were already away, thankfully.

We crept through the home and it was quiet. Something caught my eye just outside the back window. I silently waved at Jerakan and pointed to the window. He nodded and we slipped out a side door and rushed into the backyard. The burning fields were to the west, where most of the minotaurs were working to contain it.

Two alien pirates ducked behind a shed when we came around the corners of the house and we walked quickly to the sides of the shed. The South-

Taupis were smaller than minotaurs and we soon easily took hold of them.

"Think you can take our wives and children?" I roughly shook the one in my hands.

Jerakan pulled out a small chain from his pockets and used it to bind one of the alien's hands behind his back. He pitched another one to me.

"You came prepared?" I laughed as I bound the one in my hands.

"Always ready. This is a very real problem." Jerakan didn't return my laughter, but I understood. This was a grave situation.

He pushed the two of them to the ground and further secured them with rope found in the shed. "Now, where are your comrades?"

"We don't know what you're talking about," one pirate said, trying to convince us of his ignorance.

I pulled a small dagger from my belt and held it to the throat of the other. "We're not fools. Where are they? Tell us, and we'll let you live."

"Maybe we will." Jerakan did the same with his alien.

"Trust me, Taupis, we'd just as soon spill your blood and be rid of you as to keep you alive. No problem for me to slice your throat wide open."

"Too many. We scatter." Mine spoke, his boxy teeth a mess in his mouth.

Jerakan was already on his comm calling for help. "You're heading to prison or even a prison ship. Probably send you out into space without the means to do anything but float." He eyed me and I played along with it.

"Yeah, enough food for a little while. It's where we send those who won't help stop the taking of our women and children."

"We are everywhere." Jerakan's pirate spoke.

"And we'll find you everywhere. If it's the last thing we do."

The pirate spat at him.

Jerakan grabbed hold of his shirt and shook him, slightly banging his head against the wall. "You will pay for this, little one."

Help soon arrived in the form of the minotaur military. They would have the last say as to how the pirates would be treated from here on.

"We don't free them. This has to stop," Ajoe, one of the commanders, told us.

He and the other military personnel took the two South-Taupis to their holding cells until they met with the regional authorities to determine what to do with them.

We soon had teams going in four different directions to catch the others that were still in the area. Some were found up the road by another minotaur named Tekkis who had apprehended two more of them who were trying to take his wife, son, and daughter.

Jerakan and I headed straight away to the Tekkis Ranch to provide any help he might still need once we were alerted of the situation. We got there just as another pirate had pitched a burning torch into his hay field. Luckily, we were able to rush in and grab the troughs of water he had for his horses to put the fires out. One torch didn't do a lot of damage since we were there the moment they threw it into the field.

Further down the road, some South-Taupis had taken hold of a young boy halfling, the lad about four years old. He screamed and kicked, undoubtedly taught to react this way if taken. With our swords drawn, we easily rescued him.

"Where are the others?" Jerakan growled while shaking one of the Taupis.

The alien kept his mouth shut and said nothing. Jerakan shook him harder and got in his face, growling. "I will tear you limb from limb. Again, where are the others?"

This time the Taupis trembled and shook his head. "They are camped at Lunabarge."

Ah! Finally! We had an answer. Jerakan took the alien with us and I ran ahead after I saw two more of the pirates duck behind some trees. It wasn't much of a fight at that point. Their advantage had always been with numbers and diversions. Otherwise, the minotaurs could beat the life out of them. Now we had three and we would meet up with the military and hand them over.

"Lunabarge. We're heading there. Bring backup," I said to the minotaur military officer.

We headed toward Lunabarge shortly thereafter. It was a small community where the rivers joined and then forked off in different directions. The moon shone on the waters to reveal the turbulence of the streams, making it a beautiful place to behold.

"There, across the rivers." Jerakan pointed across the small lake to the corner where no minotaurs lived, but campfires lit the area. I took out my binoculars and zoomed in on the South-Taupis who were in the woods. There was a tent in the middle with humans inside.

"This is it! The wives and children are there, or at least some of them are."

"Perhaps we'll not break the legs of the one who can tell us where the rest of them have gone." Jerakan pulled up his comm and told the nearby military units about the encampment. "You may get your new wife back much sooner than expected."

I chuckled as relief flooded over me. "Yes, Auryn would like that as well." The memory of our goodbye washed over me, leaving behind a blush I couldn't contain. I missed her soft skin, her fragrance, the way she reacted when I moved a certain way. I would probably need to overtake the caravan enroute so that I could bring her home.

We apprehended just under one hundred South-Taupis that evening. They claimed the women and children in their camp were all they had and they were waiting on a small shuttle to fly in and take them. So, we set up the camp and waited while they took the aliens in for additional questioning.

"The nearest regions have agreed to help in this effort, the two territories to our west, where the South-Taupis were going. The territory to our east hasn't had any issues so far." Joil told us. He worked in the enforcement area, giving his ranch to his brother so that he could keep his human wife and three small sons safe. They lived closest to the south border, very near the Taupis territory.

I spent the night near the southern border, traveling in the caravan was faster than my old truck would have been. Perhaps I should acquire a caravan when I fetch Auryn. The South-Taupis situation began to settle down when we apprehended the nearly one hundred at Lunabarge. I wished Auryn had a comm so that I could speak with her. I remembered the driver, Ducoko, had one, so I called him.

"I'm sorry, Vrakius, Auryn ran away at the first stop we made. I would have gone after her, except I had a caravan full of women and children and couldn't do that. I called the local enforcement station and they said they'd contact you to let you know."

"Drakons. I shouldn't have sent her away. Do you know where she ran to?"

"According to the one named Catherine, she wanted to come back to Taurus Terra to find you."

There was no point in sleeping at that point. I got up to find my wife. My heart pounded as I wondered whether she was okay or if she had been captured. We had the South-Taupis under control in our area, but there was no guarantee that others were no longer present.

"Jerakan, I hate to bother you, but Auryn came back to Taurus Terra on foot. I have to find her as she's out there wandering around alone."

Jerakan sat up. "Yes, of course. Let's go."

"I'll drive while you sleep if that's alright."

I took off in the caravan and we traveled much faster with no load in the back. We zoomed through the Taurus territory with ease, and I was relieved that there were no problems this time. It took three hours of driving at top speed to finally reach my truck.

"Jerakan, call on me if you ever need a helping hand." I reached out to touch our hands in the way minotaurs greet one another.

"The same to you, Vrakius. I wish you the best with your new wife. May your seed grow your family richly."

I had to find Auryn. The first thing I needed to do was backtrack to the station where Auryn had gotten off and ask who had seen her. My eyes stayed focused on the rough terrain as I drove and left Taurus Terra. Once I did, I no longer sensed her nearby like I did while in the territory. It concerned me to travel an hour away from Taurus, and yet I had to trust my heart. After some thought, I turned around to go back home. Auryn might have already arrived into the territory and would soon be looking for my ranch. She would likely ask about my ranch and where it was located. If my heart was leading me toward my love, that's where I would go.

I kept my eyes open for any signs of Auryn on the way back to my ranch. Every spot I could do so, I pulled off and asked if they'd seen her. None had. The road I was on wasn't a direct route from the northeast corner, and that's the path she would likely have been on.

Lukie, my main ranch hand, hadn't seen her near the ranch at all. I took out my hover scooter, so that I could travel through the vast areas without worrying about needing a road for the truck. The scooter had room on the back for another rider as well as a rack for her bag. Please, heart, help me find my love.

Chapter 8

Auryn

Maybe getting off the caravan wasn't the smartest idea I've ever had. I've never hitched a ride anywhere and with the South-Taupis kidnapping humans, I was very worried about trying to catch a ride. But when a truck full of minotaurs hauling a load of farm implements into Taurus Terra asked if I needed a ride, who was I to refuse?

"Thank you so much. I'm trying to get back to my husband, Vrakius, in Taurus Terra."

"I am Neofin and this is Durrios. We're bringing equipment back to our ranches. Vrakius? We don't know him. Do you know where his ranch is?"

"He said central west. We were headed there after we married and the South-Taupis had come in and were setting fields ablaze and capturing women and children. He hurriedly put me on a caravan back east to my family there. I begged him not to do it, but I got on the caravan anyway. I just didn't feel right going away like that. I wanted to help him, so I jumped out at the first rest stop and headed back here. Even if I have to wait at the border I would feel safer as I would be closer to him."

Neofin laughed. "You women sure are headstrong. My wife, Ceila, she's like you. We live near a big lake and she'd never leave."

"Right, neither would Tiffany." There is more laughter.

I sat back. At least I had some nice minotaurs who have wives back home and understand my plight to travel with. "I'm not sure where to go, but if I could just get closer that would be helpful."

"We can get you closer, maybe even put you on a caravan heading that way. We have to get the equipment to our ranch and take this truck back, first."

"I understand. Thank you for helping me."

I sat back and listened to their banter. Me being in the cab didn't bother them at all. Once in a while, they'd ask me questions, like where I was from and what I thought of Vrakius. What could I say? It was truly love at first sight for me. We'd been together twice for such a short time and I couldn't imagine my life without him now. It was strange how fate worked. I was curious about them as well.

"May I ask, did you fall in love instantly with your wives?"

More laughter. Durrios turned to me.

"Fate is fickle, but yes. Tiffany didn't care for me so much at first, but I was all about her."

"Nah, Ceila and I felt right comfortable when we got married." Neofin nodded.

"Tiffany took a few days? Months?"

"She had no choice. We marry, we mate. It's in our

instincts. She'd tell you it took a couple of weeks. I think she started out afraid of the whole thing, and put up one of those *emotional* walls. Getting pregnant on the first time helped. With a wee one growing in her belly, she came around to loving me. And now we have two children. A girl and a boy."

My belly stirred at the mention of children and getting pregnant on the honeymoon. Wouldn't that be wild? I dozed in the backseat while we continued traveling to their ranch. Vrakius stayed in my dreams and when the truck stopped abruptly, I flung forward, calling out his name.

"Sorry, Auryn, he's not here."

I rubbed my head and smiled. "I was dreaming about him."

"We're at our ranch. We've gone as far as we can. If you want to hang around for another two days, one of us can drive you closer." Neofin smiled.

"That's very kind of you. I'm anxious and want to head that way on foot, though. I know it's far to walk, but maybe I'll find another ride down there."

"Just be very careful. If the South-Taupis are active in Taurus, you could be in danger." Durrios held out his hand to help me from the truck.

"Thank you. I will be careful."

The road south west had the sun partially in my eyes as I walked. There wasn't much traffic in these areas where they lived off the land and had no need to travel. The sky grew an angry dark gray to the southeast, a storm brewing and coming off the gulf. I had no idea what the weather was doing, whether it was a hurricane or just a small storm. I kept walking, trudging along with my bag in tow.

Soon, the sun disappeared from the clouds and large raindrops began to fall in huge drops. I had heard that in Taurus Terra as well as in the neighboring territories there could be terrible storms compared to those where I was from. A flash of lightning followed by the low rumble of thunder told me the storm was several miles away. At least, the worst part of it hadn't reached me yet.

The deluge came down in droves and wind whipped at my hair and dress, causing me to stumble. Oh, how I wished someone, anyone, would come along the deserted road. A ranch sat off from the road, the home windows lit, a small pond laid to the side and in the distance boarius and cattle mingling in the fields, safe and sound.

"Hey, lady!"

A woman ran up the road, waving a towel and shouting.

"Me?" I stopped, the rain pouring over my face, and waved back.

"Yes. Are you walking somewhere?" She kept moving toward me.

I turned and approached her as well since the rain kept me from hearing her. "Yes, I'm walking to my new husband's ranch. We got separated because of the South-Taupis."

"You poor thing. Would you like to come in and dry off while getting a bite to eat?"

I nodded. The boom of thunder added to my

willingness to follow her to her home. I could at least wait until the storm subsided before walking back out into the elements. The evening had swooped in quickly and added to the darkness.

Once inside the home, the woman handed me a towel and looked me over. "Do you have any dry clothes that you can change into? I can wash these for you. By the way, I'm Candace. These are my little darlings, Lewis, Mari, and little toot here is Winsy."

"Hi. I'm Auryn Ridge... I just married Vrakius Tarvir. He has a ranch in the west central area and I'm trying to make my way back to him."

"However did you get separated from your husband? Things are not safe with the South-Taupis out there kidnapping others. Some, I believe, are further south."

"They are near north central."

Her hand covered her mouth. "We'd heard of the raid at Lunarbarge, just a smidgen southeast of here. They apprehended many Taupis and freed the women and children they had kidnapped."

I told her how I ended up here. She listened, captivated by my story.

"Incredible. So much has been trying to pull you apart. One thing about these minotaurs, they are fiercely loyal and they protect what's theirs. If he sent you off, he thought it best for your safety. You say you had a bad feeling about leaving? I wonder if something happened to them along the way?"

Candace had a sweet motherly disposition. She was older than me, and very nurturing. Her children obeyed her wishes. I noticed they didn't have horns on their heads, but their facial features looked like minotaur. A beautiful mixture of human and minotaur.

"Ho, Daddy's home," boomed a loud voice and the back door slammed.

I whipped around just in time to see a huge minotaur walk through the door. His eyes landed on Candace and then his three wee ones. Then on me. His brow rose curiously.

"Huntagar, this is Auryn. Auryn, Huntagar." Candace smiled.

"Pleased to meet you," Huntagar said.

"Same."

"Auryn was walking to her new husband's ranch. She recently married Vrakius Tarvir." Candace explained.

Huntagar thought for a moment. "Yes. I came over here on the same ship with Vrakius."

A smile stretched across my face. "Really? He's a wonderful husband. I fell in love with him instantly."

Candace told my tale about what's going on with the South-Taupis and how Vrakius had sent me East, as well as how I followed my gut instincts and came back.

"The South-Taupas had a huge defeat today. I believe your husband was among those responsible for their downfall. They've taken over a hundred of them to the regional prison. Also, many women and children were reunited with their families."

"Oh no! Oh, no, I mean *that's good,* but that means Vrakius will be traveling east to get me, and I'm here!"

Huntagar laughed. "No worries. I'll contact him. You don't have a Taurus comm yet?"

I shook my head. "No, we had just crossed the border when all this happened." I looked down feeling defeated. Now Vrakius will be heading to the east coast to fetch me, and I won't be there. He'll be so worried.

Huntagar made a few calls while trying to locate Vrakius. "Okay, I see. Yes. Thank you, Jerakan. That's good. If you can. Yes. We'll host her until he arrives."

"Well?" My brow lifted.

"Jerakan said he found out from the caravan driver you had taken off at the first stop. He's heading back to his ranch and will move out from there, hoping to find you. If that's the case, he'll be coming through here."

"Then I need to wait on the road?"

"Jerakan said he will contact Vrakius and tell him where you are. We're to host you here until he arrives." He grinned and moved to the table, taking a seat.

"Good, it's settled then. Auryn and I are becoming good friends." Candace smiled as she set a giant pot on the table.

"Boarius stew. Have you ever had boarius?" Huntagar asked.

"I have. I like it very much. It's very pork-like with a hint of beef." I winked at Candace, who was nodding in agreement with my characterization of the food.

"Can I call her Aunt Auryn?" Lewis asked.

"Very human like, my children." Huntagar laughed.

"Yes, love, you can." Candace turned to me. "I've brought in my human traditions. I came from a very large family."

"That's nice. It was just my parents, two sisters, and me in my household while growing up. My grandparents died before I was born. And my aunts and uncles were scattered so far apart, we never got to see them. I came from a very poor family." I looked down, the shame of it weighing on me.

Candace reached across the table. "We all did. My family just happened to congregate together in the old Ohio River Valley. There are communes of humans there, but the young ladies, most anyway, choose the genetics match route. I did, and I have no regrets." She grabbed Huntagar's hand and squeezed. Their interaction warmed me. I missed Vrakius.

Chapter 9

Vrakius

The hover scooter zoomed over a small creek. I had been driving for hours, heading to the northeast corner of Taurus Terra. My comm buzzed and I pulled over to answer it.

"Jerakan, any news?"

He chuckled. "Hello, Vrakius. I have news. I know where Auryn is."

My heart pumped wildly. "Where?"

"She's at the ranch of Huntagar Vogan. They are hosting her until you arrive."

I thought for a moment. "Yes, I know Huntagar. He came over on the ship with me. I don't know for certain where he lives, though."

"I'm sending coordinates."

"Thank you, Jerakan. I will go back to my ranch and get my truck. I'm on a hover scooter right now."

"She'll be there waiting for you."

I had driven all night already, my body slammed with fatigue. As much as I wanted to be with Auryn, I needed a couple of hours of sleep before I could leave. I drove back to the ranch and took a nap. Five hours later, I awoke with a start. *Five hours!* I didn't intend on sleeping that long, but knowing Auryn was safe helped me to relax.

I jumped into the truck and headed for the Vogan ranch. They had a place sprawling along the old road with herds of boarius in the back. Cattle fields were even farther back. His cattle had long horns and this type was well known in this area.

The early morning sun peeked over my back as I parked and made my way to the door. Inside, I heard a woman calling her family for breakfast. Then I heard my mate speaking and my heart quickened.

"*Vrakius!*" Auryn squealed as the door opened and she flung herself into my arms. "I know it's only been a few days, but it feels like a lifetime." She rained kisses over my face and our lips met. I had to remind myself that we were in someone's home and little children were watching.

"This is Candace. Huntagar, her husband, has already gone out to the field. And these little ones are Lewis, Mari, and little Winsy."

Candace wiped her hands on a towel and came around the bar to say hello to me. "Huntagar is anxious to see you again." She smiled warmly. "And Auryn and I have become fast friends."

"I call her Aunt Auryn," The one named Lewis said to me.

I lifted my brow to Auryn. "Just know, I'm going to love being a minotaur rancher's wife." Her fingers curled through mine.

"You're just in time for breakfast. I have fried boarius strips, big hen eggs, and fresh patted biscuits. A mixture of southern human and minotaur foods."

I smiled. "Yes, I am well acquainted with human food being here on Alia Terra."

Auryn sat beside me and we ate a delicious meal together. She nodded as she took a bite of the boarius. "This is my new favorite meat."

I chuckled. "Good, because I don't serve beef at my house. *Ahem. Our* house." Auryn and I exchanged a loving gaze. I couldn't wait to take her into my arms and make her mine again.

"Would you like to see your old friend?" Auryn kept hold of my hand as we walked to the guest room where she slept and we gathered her bag.

"Yes, I suppose I should." I wanted to see Huntagar, but I also wanted to get Auryn home and have her to myself.

Candace led the way with her children in tow to the field. Huntagar stood near the back of the field, pitching hay into a pasture full of horses.

"Vrakius, alas! My friend." Huntagar met us half way and we greeted each other by touching our hands together.

"Wonderful to see you again, Huntagar. I see you've done well for yourself." I looked at Candace and his three young ones.

He stepped to his wife and put his arm around her. "Yes, she's the best. And we've been together for almost five years now. Just think, this will be you and Auryn in a few years."

Auryn giggled and I squeezed her to my side. "I would love that. She's certainly the center of my world now. Even if young ones do not come, I'll die a very happy minotaur."

Huntagar has a larger farm than I do. He gave me ideas to add horses as well as more boarius, since that's the staple meat of the minotaur territory.

"I would love to send some boarius jerky back home to my family." Auryn wanted to make certain her family had plenty to eat.

"Thank you for hosting my wife," I said as we loaded the truck later that afternoon.

Candace and Huntagar and their children gathered around us.

"We enjoyed having her stay with us. We don't receive many visitors here. I enjoyed getting to know you, Auryn," Candace said to my wife.

Auryn hugged her and each child before turning back to me. We settled into the truck and headed south to Tavir Ranch.

"I'm sorry that I disregarded your concern and came back here."

"It's alright. Funny thing, the caravan driver said when they reached the Carolina Terra the caravan broke down. He wouldn't have gotten you to your family after all."

"Hmm. Funny how fate works. I had a gut feeling, but I thought it was more that you needed me."

I took her hand into mine and brought it to my lips. "I do need you."

I couldn't drive the truck fast enough the few hours it took to reach our ranch. Auryn's eyes were big as she took in the fields and the animals and the home.

"I want to learn how to do everything. I want to help you in all areas."

I laughed. "You will. I will teach you all about it. I want to incorporate human traditions as well. You should feel as at home and comfortable as I do."

Her eyes took in the home as we entered. The kitchen opened to the living room. A giant fireplace separated the living space from the sleeping quarters inside. I was told to build a minimum of three bedrooms with room to add on more should I need it. At the time, I didn't have a wife. Now that I do and I can see how desirable she is, I wonder if three bedrooms will be enough.

"I love it! It's so rustic and nice. I love the woodwork, the craftsman style."

"It is minotaur style, though the home is certainly human inspired. We have one bathroom, as minotaurs only ever had one in each home on Tariat. It's a large one."

She stepped inside, her eyes going to the large stone tub. A shower hung from the wall with a 360 degree curtain wrapping around it.

"This is huge. We had the tiniest of bathrooms in our library apartment. A tiny stall shower, tiny sink and a toilet. No storage except for the shelves my dad hung over the toilet. This is massive. I wish my family could come here to see this." She turned to me with her doe-eyes peering at me.

"I would love for your family to come here, but the authorities would never allow it. I wish it were different."

"I know." She rested her head on my chest. "I can dream. Anyway, with me gone, they have it much easier. And when my sisters receive their matches they'll have it even better. Each couple receives very little allotment of food in the human colonies. Knowing my parents, they will share it with others."

The plight of humans on their home planet bothered me. Why it had to be this way made me so thankful for my kin here in the minotaur territory. We had it well with plenty of food and friendly neighbors. We helped one another whenever needs arose.

"And this is my bedroom."

"Ours." Auryn turned to me, her eyes locking with mine.

I leaned in, closing the gap between us. Our hearts pounded with desire within our chests. She moaned as I roughly grabbed her arms and moved my lips over hers. Her softness opened to me, our tongues touching, sparking a passion that would not be denied.

Her hands moved to the belt on my pants. I helped her, and sprang out of my clothes very quickly. She lifted her hands and I pulled off her dress. Kneeling, I reached for the binding behind her and unfastened the bra hiding her luscious breasts. Auryn shimmied out of her panties and standing before each other naked, we paused, just gazing into each other's eyes.

She closed the gap, her soft naked body pressing solidly into mine as we tumbled back to the bed.

My hands wandered aimlessly over her smooth skin, finding her pleasure spots, and then gently tickling her. Instantly her body reacted, her back arching as pleasure coursed through her veins and settled into her pelvis.

Auryn relaxed back onto the pillows and smiled. Her arms opened, inviting me to settle on her, her legs open. I crawled between her knees, hovering over her as I lowered on top of her, keeping most of my weight on my knees so I wouldn't hurt my love. Her arms wrapped around my neck as she lifted her head to place her lips against mine. The kiss flooded warmth to my cock, causing it to fill with blood, growing long and hard. And to think, she was all mine. I would get to have her whenever I wanted.

"Oh Vrakius, this is all I want. This, right now, right here. You with me." Her lips moved over mine, her hand moving over my back, nails digging into me.

"I love you, Auryn Tavir. You are mine." Our kisses grew in intensity, as if we were starved for the other, like it would be the last kiss between us.

She groaned as my hand trailed down her body. To start the moment, I wanted to watch her lose herself with me. I wanted to take in the ecstasy on her face as she came as a result of my hand. It caused my cock to grow so hard, I could barely contain myself.

Auryn moaned, her head rolling to the side as I lowered my head and sucked on a taut nipple.

Chapter 10

Auryn

Vrakius tenderly brought me to the heights of pleasure that left me panting for air and wanting more. Always wanting more. I couldn't get enough of him. My need for release blew through my body like someone shot an arrow that tore from one end to the other. The tremors started in my lower belly and fanned out, down my legs, and to the tips of my toes. My body exploded as his giant hand stayed between my legs, his fingers moving through my soft warm slit, swirling over my clit. His lips gently sucked my nipple.

"Oh yes! *YES!*" My back arched upward and the moans were so loud that I knew the others living near the ranch could hear me. Being in his arms, having Vrakius watch as I lost complete control, was all I wanted in the world.

My body rocked through the pleasure as if I was soaring through the stars, the very air I breathed igniting the fire that burned hot. Slowly, I came down and shoved his hand away, collapsing back onto the pillows.

Vrakius hovered over me, his body rigid, ready to claim me. I reached for him, drawing his face to mine, our lips pressing together, tongues darting back and forth. He consumed me with his mouth, his hands sliding over my bare skin. My legs wrapped around his waist as I lifted my pelvis. I was wet and ready to receive him, healed from losing my virginity, and so ready to have him inside me.

"I love you." Vrakius took his throbbing cock and swirled it between my legs. Pleasure sparked again as I ground into him.

"I want you inside me. Claim me, Vrakius. Make me yours."

He groaned as he pressed his huge cock through the opening of my slick tunnel. I stretched around him, but instead of the searing pain I had felt the first time, this time my body warmed, wanting it, needing it.

Slowly, his cock filled me, stretched me. I moaned as he sawed all the way in and then back out, until just his head was at the entrance. He groaned, his strong arm holding me. Leaning down, our lips smashed together in a passionate kiss as he moved in and out of me. My body ground into the bed and lifted meeting with his thrusts. His huge cock rubbed against my swollen clit, making me lose control all over again.

Our bodies moved in unison, both of us moaning, lost in the moment, lost in the pleasure that joined our souls and brought us to the peak of the mountain. We soared together as my pelvis exploded. I clung to him, my nails digging into his back. My back arched.

He lurched forward, thrusting hard. His cock filled me completely, giving me what I wanted so badly. I desired a baby and I wanted a family. We held onto each other, as pleasure rushed through us, taking us from peak to peak.

I let out a deep breath as he thrusted deep inside me one last time. We clung to the other, our lips moving together as we parted and gasped for air. He held himself above me, resting on his hands, his cock still inside me. I squeezed my tunnel and he groaned, his eyes smiling down at me. Our lips met again, the passion not yet fully extinguished. Slowly, Vrakius pulled out and rolled to the side and onto his back.

We laid silently while holding hands and merely breathing. Contentment came over me in huge waves. I could stay here like this forever. The subtle aftershocks of such a powerful orgasm rocked throughout my body. My heart was full of love. I turned to him, smiling. My hand traced the angles of his face and horns through his long locks of hair.

"How are you, my love?" His deep voice settled deep into my soul, connecting with me. A voice I wanted to hear for the rest of my life.

"Perfect. Absolutely perfect."

He rolled to me, pulling me into his arms. We laid there so long that we drifted to sleep. Both of us were tired from the stress of being apart, from all the wandering and driving. We were finally in total contentment in each others' arms.

I woke up hours later and Vrakius had rolled over

and was snoring softly, so I went to the bathroom and took my first shower in the stone tub. Then, I filled the tub with hot water and sank down. When I was a little girl my family lived in a tiny apartment that had a bathtub. I took baths with my sisters and we loved it. Now, I had the luxury of a larger tub and the quiet of the ranch. Outside the only sounds were lowing from the cattle. Even the boarius piled together and slept soundly.

The steamy water relaxed me so much that I dozed again.

"What's my love doing? Drifting in the tub?" Vrakius stood by the tub, still naked, his face stretched into a brilliant smile.

"Oh, yes. Sorry. I showered, then I wanted to try the tub. Join me. I'll refresh with hot water."

He sat down opposite me, his huge legs bent. The tub, while large for me, wasn't quite big enough for him to stretch out. The cooler water drained half way and we refilled it with hot water. My fingers were shriveled, but I didn't care. For so long I'd traveled and the quick shower at Huntagar and Candace's place had not relaxed me so well.

"Come here, you're too far away."

I spun around and relaxed against Vrakius as we let the hot steamy water turn us into wet noodles. His hardness bobbed at my backside playfully and his fingers reached around, resting on my breasts. I giggled as he moaned softly in my ears.

"I'm ready for another round."

I turned around, situating myself on him, facing

him and leaning in for a kiss. I pulled back, giggling again and grabbed the sponge on the ledge and soaped it.

"You're a dirty boy, I need to clean you first."

He moaned as I took my time washing his massive body. His cock elongated in my soapy hands and he grabbed them as I was rubbing vigorously.

"No, not like this," he growled.

I giggled and rinsed my hands. "No worries. You're clean."

My brow lifted as I grabbed a towel and dried while the water drained in the tub. He lunged at me as I walked out of the bathroom, grabbing me to him. Outside, the moon rose and cast silvery light through the windows. Otherwise, the place would have been dark. We stumbled back to the bedroom and he laid on the bed, opening his arms to me.

"My turn." I hopped on the bed and crawled on top of him, straddling his middle.

Leaning down, our lips met. No matter how much we kissed, I wanted more. I *needed* more. His strong arms wrapped around my body, hands rubbing down my back and grabbing my buttocks and squeezing.

"You're mine, Auryn. All mine."

"Forever." I touched the tip of my nose to him and he chuckled. Then he grabbed me, landing his lips on mine in a kiss that would have knocked me off my feet if I weren't already lying on top of him.

"Pinch me," I said.

"What? Why would I do that, my love?" His brow

furrowed.

I laughed. "It's a figure of speech humans use. It means to make certain I'm not dreaming. This is real. *You* are real."

He bucked up showing me just how real and at attention he was. I lifted my body, and guided him to me. Slowly, I sat and allowed his giant cock to fill me once again. He cocked a brow.

"Oh."

I smiled and slowly moved up and down over him while being in control. Leaning forward, I brought my lips to his while I rocked my pelvis. Our kisses burned with passion, unrelenting, inextinguishable. Truely, I could do this all the time. Making love to him became my most favorite thing in the world. The rest of the world could wait while we savored each other, enjoying every little moan, touch, release of energy.

"I love you, Vrakius. I never dreamed it was possible to fall so deeply in love so fast." I moaned as I leaned forward, allowing the friction against my clit.

"Powerful fate. If humans had fated mates it would be this quick. You're mine, undoubtedly." He breathed quickly, his hands grabbing my hips and helping me move.

"Humans do experience this. Just not very often. But this, this fate stuff. This DNA stuff, oh wow. How wonderful."

Suddenly, my body exploded. I ground into him, my back arching. He helped me, his hands grasping my hips and moving me to his satisfaction. Vrakius groaned and lurched forward, his hips moving with mine, filling me. Pleasure rushed over us to the point I nearly passed out. If it weren't for him holding onto me, I would have fallen over.

I laid on his chest, his cock still embedded inside me. His arms wrapped around my back, rubbing me.

"I love you, my mate."

I lifted my face after the dizziness passed. "I love you, too." Our lips met again.

Rolling to the side of him, I curled up, deeply lethargic and happy. We fell asleep wrapped in each other's arms and woke up well after the sun was high in the sky.

He jumped up with a start. "A rancher can't sleep the day away."

I reached for him. "Don't you have a ranch hand helping?"

"Of course."

"Then he understands that you just got home with me. We're still *honeymooning*." I sat up and rubbed his back.

He turned to me, pulling me into his strong arms. "You're right."

"We will work together from now on." I was in this for life and I aimed to learn everything there is to learn about being a rancher. It's a far cry difference from the dilapidated city in which I grew up.

Chapter 11

Vrakius

Auryn fell in step with the ranch learning all the jobs. Every day she woke with me as the sun rose. Together we cooked the meals, tended the farm, and fell into bed each night enraptured with our love.

She slept in this morning, and I didn't have the heart to rouse her from what looked like a deep sleep. Instead, I cooked boarius strips and eggs hoping the aroma would entice her. When she didn't show up in the kitchen, I walked into the bedroom to find the bed empty. The sound of retching came from the bathroom.

"My love, are you ill?" I walked in without knocking.

She looked up, her face sweating. "Hand me a wet cloth, please."

"You are pale. I insist you go back to bed. I'll bring you something to drink." I wet down the cloth and gave it to her.

Auryn stood and managed a smile. "I'm famished."

My mouth hung open as I followed her out the door. She went from dreadfully sick to hungry within a few seconds.

"This is so good. Wow. Oh, do you have coffee? Actual coffee? Coffee was rare back east. May I?" Auryn made no sense. She was bubbly and all about the food.

"Coffee came to us from way south. The humans down there grow it. The aliens down there trade with us for cattle." I laughed at the absurdity of it.

"Mmmm." She belched and sat back, rubbing her stomach while frowning.

I grabbed her arm. "Are you okay? You were ill and then you ate like you were starved and now you're ill once again?"

She shook her head as tears filled her eyes. At the very same moment she began to laugh. "Vrakius, I think I might be pregnant. We've been together for a month and a half since we married and I haven't had my monthly cycle. I know it can happen, but me? I'm a wife and now a mother. A mother to a minotaur halfling. Wild!"

I was stunned. I knelt beside her and wrapped my arms around her. She turned to me, burying her head into my shoulder. "This is what we want, remember?" My hand smoothed her hair down her back.

Pulling back, Auryn locked her teary eyes with mine. "I'm sorry, Vrakius. I think it's the hormones. So much has changed for me over the past couple of months. This has been a whole new life that I jumped into head first to live. And now this. This cements it. Can we visit Candace and Huntagar?

She's done this three times and I have no idea where to go or what to do."

"We can make a visit to the Vogan ranch. There are midwives around this area and some of the wives use them. I'm sure we can find one near us."

Worry lines filled her forehead. "What if I need medical help?"

"There are medical facilities with both minotaur healers and human doctors and nurses nearby as well. Don't worry, I will take good care of you and our little one."

Candace ran outside the moment we arrived and threw her arms around my mate. My heart swelled with happiness seeing how receptive Auryn was to her. I realized she needed a good human friend like this.

"Come on in. I have some tests," Candace said while producing one of them in her hand.

Auryn looked at me nervously. "Come with me. This is your moment, too."

In the bathroom, she took the test and laid the stick on the counter. One minute was the promised results. I didn't want to watch it so I took her into my arms.

"My love, no matter what we see on that stick, I have never been happier in my entire life. Just having you with me is all I ever wanted."

She nodded. "Children would be a gift on top of that."

We turned around and looked at the test. It had a large plus sign in the result window. No more guesswork was necessary.

"Oh my! Vrakius! We're going to be parents!"

I chuckled and embraced her. "I already thought so."

The rest of the visit was all about what to expect during the pregnancy as well as during labor and birth. Huntagar raised a brow and motioned for me to follow him outside and leave the two women to their giddy conversations.

"Congratulations! Just some advice, though. Human women get very emotional during this time."

"Hormones." I nodded and we laughed. "I'm already experiencing it."

He placed his hand on my shoulder. "Just go along with it. Be there, hug her often, give her what she craves, and let her cry and laugh at will."

"I was born for this," I said with more conviction than I ever thought I'd have. "She is my fated mate and now we've made a baby. This is my job, to be her husband as well as a father."

"Next spring, we are planning a trip back to Tariat. You and your wife and new baby are welcome to come along."

"A winter baby. Yes, that makes sense. Thank you for the offer. I'll speak with Auryn about it. I'm certain she'd love to see it, but is it safe for our women and children to travel there?"

"Perfectly. My brother, Hagan, has taken his wife and son multiple times. And the first time she traveled, their son was two weeks old." It was good to have another minotaur with whom to speak about such things. It made me glad to be able to share thoughts with Huntagar.

Days later, we saw a midwife near the ranch. Bethany had two children of her own with her minotaur husband, Jute.

"She's perfectly healthy. The baby is due in January, towards the end. And from what I can hear, there's just one in there."

Auryn looked at me with wide eyes. "Just one. I can't imagine having more than one."

"I've seen it." Bethany's blond hair bounced as she nodded. She and Jute had two blond headed daughters who both looked more like bethany.

Auryn is such a beautiful creature. I wouldn't mind if our child took after her more than me.

"We need to make a nursery. I want the baby with us for the first year." She stood in our bedroom sizing up a corner.

"What do we need? Anything, you name it. I'll buy it or make it."

She giggled. "Aren't you a doting hubby? First, we need a crib, a place to lay the baby once he or she is here. We need diapers, but I believe Bethany will teach me how to make my own. We'll need clothes. There's a swap bazaar in the community up the road, so we can join it and find all the baby items we need there. I will breastfeed, of course. It will be fine." Auryn nodded as if she had to convince herself.

"Candace said the first baby is the most challenging. Once we get the hang of this the next babies will be easy."

"If we have more."

I really hoped we would. "If we have more. I'm thankful for you and for this one right now." My hand rubbed over her swollen belly.

The summer gave way to fall with its beautiful colors. My mate blossomed with the pregnancy, her belly growing large. We enjoyed all the firsts, the baby moving, her weight gain, as well as the end to her sensitive stomach in the mornings.

Auryn cried one morning over a bowl of oatmeal.

"What is it, my love?" I rushed to her side remembering the wise words from Huntagar.

"I'm so fat. I've never weighed this much. You probably won't find me attractive once this baby comes." She spooned in a mouth full of oatmeal and began to move it around in her mouth.

"Oh, my love. You must know, I find you so attractive like this. You were so thin when we married that I was worried about your health. Don't let weight concern you. I will love you no matter what."

She sighed in my embrace. "I'm a mess, huh?"

"You are a new mother, you are beautiful, and I love you. Every single bit of you."

"I love you, too, Vrakius. I'm sorry I'm a ball of emotions these days."

We stopped making love until the baby came, a suggestion from the midwife who last saw her. Since minotaurs are so much larger than human males, the babies are larger as well.

"I can't wait to meet our little one. It won't be long, now. Bethany said the baby has dropped."

The *wait and watch* began. That's what Huntagar called it. When the baby is ready the baby will come. It wasn't as if we could set an appointment and have the baby appear at the appointed time. Bethany was just a call away and she told us she didn't see any reason why Auryn couldn't have a safe and healthy delivery.

"Candace wants to be here, too. Is that okay?" Auryn sat back, her swollen feet lifted onto a pillow, her hand rubbing over her huge belly.

"Anyone you want here is perfectly okay with me. I actually feel better knowing you'll have the support of those who have been there for you already."

Auryn grew increasingly tired and having to use the toilet every half hour didn't help. She sat up in the middle of the night, her hand on her back.

"Ouch. I'm so ready for this baby to come." When she stood on her feet, water suddenly poured out from between her legs onto the floor.

"Oh no! Oh! Call Bethany and tell her my water just broke. Oh, I'm so sorry about the mess." She rushed to the bathroom.

Like a ship taking off, my heart beat wildly as I contacted both Bethany and Candace. After giving me instructions on what to do, Candace said she would be at our house within the half-hour. I put the proper blankets on the bed, blankets to save the mattress from the blood and fluids and continued to care for my wife as best I could. We had items in a trunk ready for Auryn to give birth.

"Look at you, preparing for the birth." Auryn stood beside the bed, trembling.

My arms wrapped around her. "Bethany and Candace are on their way, too."

"Oh, Vrakius, I'm so nervous."

In truth, I was nervous as well, but I needed to be strong for her. "It will be okay. You can do this. I will be by your side the entire time."

"I love you. I'm so glad you're the father of my baby." She was so tired that her eyes were closing as she spoke.

"I love you too, Auryn. Rest as much as you can. I'm here."

Chapter 12

Auryn

Labor is just that, *labor*. I panted through the contractions and slept in between them. I thought I'd be wide awake and terribly excited. In a way, I was, but I was also extremely exhausted. Both Candace and Bethany told me to sleep as much as I could, that the real work would begin once the baby arrived.

In the quiet moments when they left me in the room to rest for ten or so minutes, I rolled to my side, hugging my belly, enjoying, if possible, the last moments of pregnancy. I've had the baby with me for nine long months. Once the baby is here, I'll have to share him or her with the world.

The pain doubled me over, hitting me so hard with so much pressure. "Oh! *OH!*"

The door flung open with Vrakius in the lead followed by Bethany and Candace. I'd labored half the night and well into the afternoon. Bethany checked me.

"Show time, everyone!" She beamed at me as she perched at the end of the bed. "Now, remember, Auryn, if you can stand and squat, gravity will help you."

Fatigue had kept me napping. Suddenly I had a burst of energy to help me get up. "Yes, help me." Vrakius and Candace got on either side of me, helping me to squat on the bed. The soft mattress nearly toppled me. "Let me get on the floor."

In a flash, Bethany dropped a waterproof blanket down and Candace helped set up pillows in case I wanted to lie down. Vrakius helped me to the floor and Candace resumed her spot beside me, just in time for a huge contraction hit.

"Yes! That's the power of gravity. Very good. Push, Auryn. Push."

I pushed with all my might. The contraction soon subsided and I relaxed against Vrakius, still squatting. If it weren't for him and Candace, I couldn't do it. They held onto me as another contraction began.

"Yes! I see a head. Lots of curly hair. Oh my. Come on, Auryn, push!"

The contraction stopped and then another came on and I pushed. The baby slid out from between my legs with Bethany catching them. Immediately a lusty cry filled the air and we all cried and laughed.

"It's a *boy!*"

"Oh! Vrakius, we have a son! A *son!*"

He and Candace lowered me onto the floor against the pillows. Bethany handed me my son. He had a head of curly brown hair and his little face looked like Vrakius. Even so, his eyes were more like mine. He was a perfect mixture of the two of us.

"Oh, he's absolutely beautiful." Vrakius took him

when I offered and held him, his misty eyes looking into his little face.

"What's his name?" Candace smiled at us, taking a picture with her comm.

"Dario Tavir." Vrakius proudly announced.

"It's one of my favorite names. And he insisted on giving our first child a human name. We'll name the next one a minotaur name."

Candace laughed. "All three of mine have human names. The minotaur territory is full of human and minotaur names."

Bethany nodded. "Many combine them."

"Interesting," I said as I reached for Vrakius. He hugged me.

"I think since she's the one that does all the work getting the baby here, she should be the one to choose the name."

"That's very sweet. You're among a minority. It's often an area of contention for couples," Bethany explained.

We settled in with our baby boy. Dario brought light and life into our home, the complete joy of our hearts. I enjoyed every moment of it, the night time feedings and diaper changes, the laundry, the visits to the swap bazaar and to my friends, especially Candace.

"Would you like to travel to Tariat on the first of March?" Vrakius was serious.

I bounced Dario on my shoulder while waiting for his little burp after his feeding. "Travel into outer space?"

"To see my home world."

I looked down, worried about the ranch and the safety of traveling with a baby. "I don't know. What will happen here? I love our home and the ranch."

"I will leave it in my capable ranch hand's care. He can run it for a season."

"A season? We'll be gone all spring?"

"About three months, yes. It takes a while to get there and then to travel back. It's not a fast trip. And that's with FTL and wormhole jumps. Would you like to know the best news?"

"What?" I bounced up and down.

"We'll be traveling with Huntagar, Candace and their children!"

I squealed. "Yes! Then let's go! Oh wow, what do I pack?"

"Talk to Candace. They've made the trip before."

So many exciting things happened to me this past year and now a trip into outer space! It topped everything I've done, well, except for marrying Vrakius and having sweet Dario. I wrote to my family back east and sent photos. I looked down sadly, thinking of how it seemed impossible to take our son to meet his grandparents, who were on the same planet and same land mass while we're talking about flying away for a season.

"What about seeing my family first? It's easier to get to mine. And then we could go."

"We'll go to Tariat and I promise we'll go when we come back."

"It's just that traveling in space and at faster than

light through wormholes can have its risks. It's a long way. I would love to show my family Dario before we go. We could take the shuttle."

He looked at me for a moment. And for a moment, I thought he'd say no. But instead, he smiled brilliantly. "Okay. Anything for you, my love."

Vrakius has always made good on his promises to me. Within a week we took off in a shuttle and landed near the city where I was born and raised.

"Look Dario, this is part of your heritage." He was barely seven weeks old. His big eyes took in the surroundings around us. We left so quickly that I didn't have time to let my parents know. They didn't own a comm and the only way to communicate was through old-fashioned letters.

Heading into the city took me back in time. So much had changed in my life over the past year. And here I was back at my beginning.

"Wow." Vrakius couldn't find the words to describe the dilapidated buildings where the humans lived. He knew it was bad, but this shocked him.

"This is us," I said as we pulled up to the old library that had been converted to apartments. Statues of old stone gargoyles were outside the entrance. Funny thing was, gargoyles were real and they lived on our planet as aliens. I didn't know much about them, but I knew they were on Alia Terra along with the minotaurs and other beings.

My mother answered the door. She looked old, worn out. Her eyes blinked for a moment as she didn't seem to recognize me.

"Mom! It's me, Auryn!"

"Oh, honey. Of course it is. Please, come in. You brought your new family here?" Her eyes widened as if I had done something bad.

"Yes. He wanted to meet you. And we wanted you to meet your grandson."

"Auryn! Oh my fuzzy bunny! It's really you!" Agnes jumped into my arms, my youngest sister always full of life.

"Meet Dario, your nephew."

"Wow. Already. And this is Mr. Minotaur. Does he have a brother?"

"Always my Agnes, always the flirt." I ruffled her hair.

"Chelsea left us three months ago. She wed a bear shifter and moved west."

"Seriously? A *bear shifter?*" I'd heard everything at this point.

"Hi, I'm Vrakius. The, uh, *minotaur.*"

I laughed. "I'm so sorry. Yes, this is my wonderful husband and the father of my baby, Vrakius Tarvir."

My mother sat down with little Dario, he was still so tiny that he snuggled into her arms. I looked around.

"Where's Dad?"

Mother and Agnes looked at each other quickly. "He's out scouting for food." Mother's shoulders slumped.

"We brought food. Vrakius." My husband opened one of his bags and dumped it in the middle of the living room floor.

Agnes bent down quickly as if she had gone for days without food.

"*Mmmf.* Whaf is it?"

"Agnes, don't talk with your mouth full." Mother admonished her, but quickly reached down and grabbed one of the packets, opening it.

"Boarius jerky. Meat from Vrakius' home planet of Tariat."

The door opened and Dad came through with his arms full of bags.

"Well, look who showed up. Auryn, my first born. And who's this?"

I laughed and hugged Dad and proudly showed him my baby. "This is your grandson, Dario. And this is Vrakius, my husband."

It was an amazing visit once Dad came home. Great bittersweetness washed over me as we left later that day as well. I knew they hadn't delivered the letters I had written to my family the entire time.

We left with promises of coming back as soon as we could. I didn't tell them about the season of travel ahead, it would just make them worry. The shuttle took us back to the ranch. The trip to Tariat would be a lifetime adventure for me.

"I hope Agnes can find her a minotaur like I have. She's always been partial to your kind. She was so jealous when I received the letter about the match."

Vrakius held our son up. Dario smiled into his father's face. He was just so precious.

We met Huntagar and Candace at the shuttle that will take us to the ship orbiting Alia Terra. The trip of a lifetime awaited us. On a spaceship with friends and with the two most favorite beings in the galaxy, Vrakius and my son, we headed into the stars.

Not an ounce of regret flowed through my veins as we arrived back on Alia Terra in July. It took a little longer due to an issue with the mother ship. However, we made it back safe and healthy. Little Dario had begun to attempt to sit up and even stand at this point. He was a little more advanced than most human babies. The minotaur blood was strong in his veins.

We brought back Vozak, Vrakius's younger brother. He came to Alia Terra to help on the ranch and to put his blood in the DNA Registry in hopes of finding a match. I can't help but secretly hope the match will indeed be my sister, Agnes. Wouldn't that be a wonderful thing?

Eden Ember

Eden Ember found her passion in writing sci-fi romance. She spends her days either pounding on the keyboard or dreaming up the next stories. Her active imagination never lets up and the perfect outlet comes through in her books.

Join Eden Ember's exclusive reader's list
- New Books, Hot Sales, and Freebies
- Eden's reader giveaways
- EXCLUSIVE sneak peeks at upcoming novels
- First look at Covers
- Who Eden Recommends (Love me some SCI FI Romance!)

EdenEmber.com
Eden Ember on FaceBook
Follow Eden Ember on Amazon
Follow Eden Ember on BookBub

Arranged Monster Mates

Wed to the Ice Giant by Layla Fae
Wed to the Wolfman by Cara Wylde

Printed in Dunstable, United Kingdom